Maine

New Hampshire

Vermont

Massachusetts

New York

Rhode Island

Connecticut

New Jersey

Delaware

Maryland

Minnesota

North Dakota

South Dakota

Wisconsin

Michigan

Pennsylvania

Iowa

Nebraska

Indiana

Ohio

Illinois

West Virginia

Virginia

Kansas

Missouri

Kentucky

North Carolina

Tennessee

Oklahoma

Arkansas

South Carolina

Mississippi

Alabama

Georgia

Texas

Louisiana

Florida

Washington, D.C.

The Twelve Days of Christmas in Washington, D.C.

written by
Candice Ransom

illustrated by
Sarah Hollander

STERLING
New York / London

Dear Olivia,

   Guess what city is in the United States but isn't in any state? If you guessed Washington, D.C., you're right! Congress created the District of Columbia, a separate city, for the U.S. capital back in 1791. (One guy wanted to call it "Washingtonople!")

   For Christmas, Mom and I are giving you a train ticket to our hometown. Since I live here, I already know D.C. is the coolest place in the country. The nation's capital belongs to everyone in the United States. So why not spend Christmas vacation visiting your city?

   It's the perfect time to visit. D.C. is decorated for Christmas from top to bottom. I have twelve special gifts for you, one for each of the twelve days of Christmas, and the first one SINGS! You'll see monuments and memorials and museums . . . and me!

   All aboard! The fun starts the minute you get off the train!

   Your favorite cousin,
   James

Dear Mom and Dad,

I'm here! James and Aunt Doris whisked me from the train to the car. We whizzed up and down busy streets. Then we walked across a footbridge over the Potomac River to a wooded island!

"Here comes your first Christmas present," James said. "His name is Ted." A spotted brown bird swooped down and landed on the branch of an oak tree. Aunt Doris says the scarlet oak tree is the official tree of Washington, D.C. James told me the leaves were as red as a firecracker just a month ago—they turn brown for the winter. The wood thrush, D.C.'s symbolic bird, is known for its beautiful song. It can sing two notes at once!

Ted led the way around Theodore Roosevelt Island. Our 26th president created the U.S. Forest Service, 5 national parks, and 51 bird sanctuaries. Purchased in 1932, this 88-acre island was dedicated in 1967 to the man who believed in saving land and wildlife. More trees for Ted to nest in!

Jets roared overhead from nearby Ronald Reagan National Airport but we still saw a raccoon and two muskrats. Animals make their homes anywhere, even near the city!

Cool!
Olivia

Hi, Mom and Dad.

This morning my muddy sneakers were gone. In their place was a pair of glittery red slippers from Aunt Doris!

I got to wear them to the Smithsonian National Museum of American History, where Dorothy's ruby slippers from the 1939 movie <u>The Wizard of Oz</u> are on display. Did you know that in the book by L. Frank Baum, the original slippers were silver? (Red shoes just showed up better in movies.)

There are more than 3 million items in this museum, including one of Thomas Edison's first light bulbs, and Prince's electric guitar! I tap-danced to the "Star-Spangled Banner" as we stared at the flag that flew over Baltimore during the War of 1812. This flag is the one that inspired Francis Scott Key to write his famous song.

James liked the shiny Model T Ford from 1913 and Abraham Lincoln's top hat (Honest Abe kept notes for speeches, letters, even bills in it). My favorite was the 23-room dollhouse containing around one thousand miniatures. It's "owned" by Mr. and Mrs. Doll, their 10 children, and 20 pets! I'd move in if I could. James clicked his heels and joked, "There's no place like home."

Not homesick yet!
Olivia

Dear Mom and Dad,

What are black and white and cute all over? Giant pandas, the stars of the National Zoo!

Mei Xiang and Tian Tian originally came from China. They're the proud parents of Tai Shan, who was born in the zoo—a very rare thing to happen! (Giant pandas are one of the world's rarest animals. The zookeeper told us that people are working hard to save them from extinction.) The baby panda is all grown up and lives in China now, but he was no bigger than a stick of butter when he was born. Each panda eats more than 50 pounds of bamboo a day. That's like us eating breakfast, lunch, and dinner ten times a day!

We also caught a quick look at a red panda with a long, fluffy, striped tail. Red pandas eat bamboo, too, but not NEARLY as much as their more famous distant cousins.

Next we saw elephants splashing around in their baths. The youngest one played with a big plastic box. He made a lot of noise—just like James!

We watched black-tailed prairie dogs pop out of holes in their "town." They aren't really dogs—they're rodents that live in colonies of tunnels. One prairie dog stood on his hind legs and watched <u>us</u>. Who was in the zoo?

Panda-crazy,

Olivia

On the third day of Christmas,
my cousin gave to me . . .

3 cute bears

2 ruby slippers,
and a thrush in a scarlet oak tree.

Mom and Dad, get on your marks!

Today was the Monument Marathon! First we raced to the Washington Monument. The elevator zipped us to the top (555 feet) in 70 seconds. We could see all the way to Arlington National Cemetery and the Pentagon across the Potomac River in Virginia.

Next we ran down the National Mall. It's a big lawn with a long, skinny pool, not a shopping center! We walked along the Vietnam Veterans Memorial, built to honor men and women who died in the Vietnam War. More than 58,000 names are engraved in the black granite wall. People leave flowers, stuffed animals, and letters. I touched the smooth, cool wall.

The Lincoln Memorial honors our 16th president, who freed the slaves during the Civil War. Abraham Lincoln's statue is over 19 feet high. James and I stared at Lincoln's craggy face and didn't speak. It was that kind of place.

Later Aunt Doris drove us around the Tidal Basin, past the Jefferson Memorial. The white-domed building looked so pretty lit against the night sky. We could see the statue of Jefferson inside. Best of all, we didn't have to walk anymore!

Worn out in Washington,

Olivia

Lincoln Memorial

On the fourth day of Christmas, my cousin gave to me . . .

4 monuments

Washington Monument

Vietnam Veterans Memorial

Jefferson Memorial

3 cute bears, 2 ruby slippers, and a thrush in a scarlet oak tree.

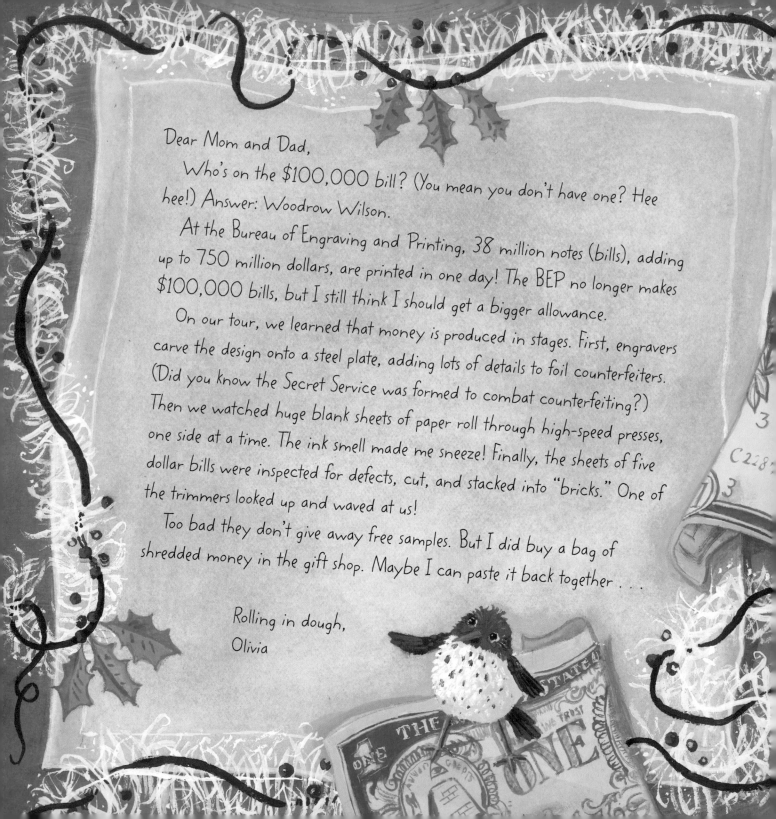

Dear Mom and Dad,

Who's on the $100,000 bill? (You mean you don't have one? Hee hee!) Answer: Woodrow Wilson.

At the Bureau of Engraving and Printing, 38 million notes (bills), adding up to 750 million dollars, are printed in one day! The BEP no longer makes $100,000 bills, but I still think I should get a bigger allowance.

On our tour, we learned that money is produced in stages. First, engravers carve the design onto a steel plate, adding lots of details to foil counterfeiters. (Did you know the Secret Service was formed to combat counterfeiting?) Then we watched huge blank sheets of paper roll through high-speed presses, one side at a time. The ink smell made me sneeze! Finally, the sheets of five dollar bills were inspected for defects, cut, and stacked into "bricks." One of the trimmers looked up and waved at us!

Too bad they don't give away free samples. But I did buy a bag of shredded money in the gift shop. Maybe I can paste it back together . . .

Rolling in dough,
Olivia

On the fifth day of Christmas,
my cousin gave to me . . .

5 dollar bills

4 monuments, 3 cute bears, 2 ruby slippers,
and a thrush in a scarlet oak tree.

Hey, Mom and Dad,

D.C. has zillions of statues. It also has zillions of squirrels. In Lafayette Park, we passed statues of General Andrew Jackson (also a president), and General Lafayette (not a president). But the squirrels stole the show. Not ordinary gray squirrels like we have at home, but black ones.

There's a mystery about these black squirrels. When Teddy Roosevelt was president (1901 to 1909), hardly any squirrels were left in D.C. due to hunting. Someone sent 18 black squirrels from Canada to the National Zoo. The squirrels got out! Soon they were all over the city, but they really liked Lafayette Park. People put up squirrel houses and special squirrel water fountains.

Now there are too many squirrels. One report says Lafayette Park has more squirrels than any place in the world. Lafayette Park has been a racetrack, an apple orchard, a graveyard, and a private zoo for President Grant (who was also a general). I think it should be called Squirrel Park!

Nuts for D.C.!

Olivia

On the sixth day of Christmas,
my cousin gave to me . . .

6 frisky squirrels

5 dollar bills, 4 monuments, 3 cute bears, 2 ruby slippers,
and a thrush in a scarlet oak tree.

Dear Mom and Dad,

James and I got all dressed up. Then we climbed the steps of the U.S. Capitol building. In the Rotunda, Aunt Doris pointed out a super famous painting, which tells part of the story of why we have a capital city. . . and a United States.

Seven men gather around a desk. Thomas Jefferson, Benjamin Franklin, and others present the Declaration of Independence they have just drafted. (Aunt Doris says that "drafting" is just a fancy way of saying that they all helped to write it.) Later, most of the men in the painting will sign the Declaration with their quill pens made out of real feathers. Some people think that John Hancock made his signature extra big because he wanted to be sure that King George over in England would be able to read it without putting his glasses on!

In the National Statuary Hall, statues of heroes from a lot of different states circle the huge room. Our guide showed us a neat trick. James stood way across the hall and I turned my back. I heard him whisper "bean soup" perfectly clear! The hall is sometimes called the "whispering gallery."

Aunt Doris got special permission to take us to the fancy Senate Dining Room. I ate a big bowl of Senate Bean Soup, served every day. Yum!

Love,
Olivia

Dear Mom and Dad,

Today I traded in my ruby slippers for ice skates and we headed for the Sculpture Garden, part of the National Gallery of Art. Every winter, the big circular fountain is frozen into a skating rink.

Huge weird statues and sculptures by famous artists squat around the rink. I practiced figure eights in front of a gigantic metal spider and did sit-spins by an enormous bright red "horse." James and I tried skating to Ted's double-tune, but we fell down a lot!

Cold and tired, we nibbled pizza in the glass-walled café. Then we went back outside and watched Ted sing from the top of "Chair Transformation," a sculpture of stacked chairs that look like they're leaning back and springing forward at the same time. We played tag around a house that was really an optical illusion, a funny long-eared rabbit on a rock, and a mammoth typewriter eraser. (Aunt Doris says that people typed on these old-fashioned machines before computers were invented.) My next art project will be <u>really</u> big!

Love,
Olivia

On the eighth day of Christmas,
my cousin gave to me . . .

8 wacky
statues

7 drafters dancing, 6 frisky squirrels, 5 dollar bills,
4 monuments, 3 cute bears, 2 ruby slippers,
and a thrush in a scarlet oak tree.

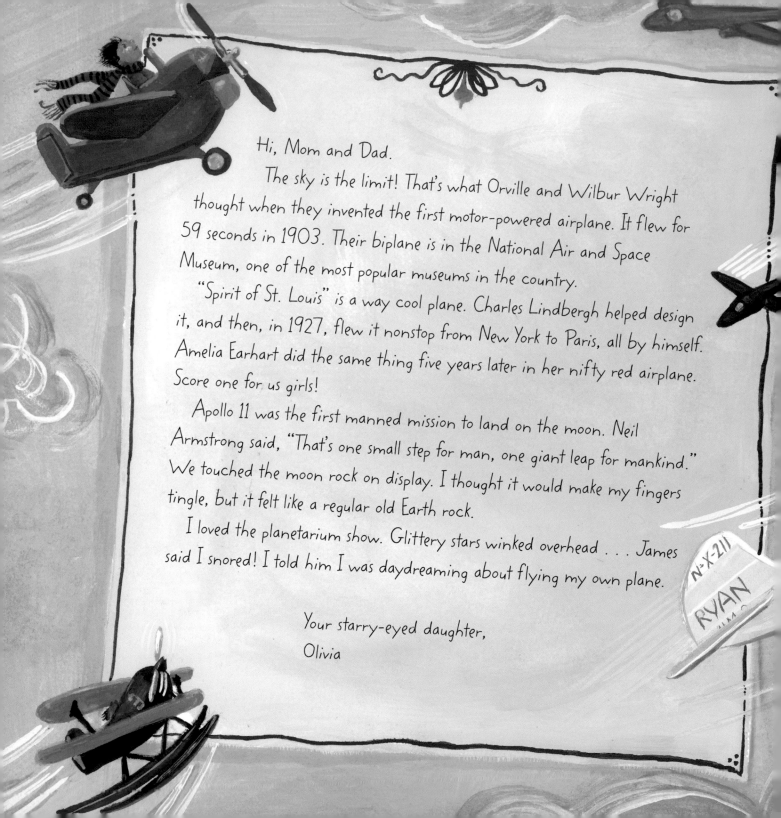

Hi, Mom and Dad.

The sky is the limit! That's what Orville and Wilbur Wright thought when they invented the first motor-powered airplane. It flew for 59 seconds in 1903. Their biplane is in the National Air and Space Museum, one of the most popular museums in the country.

"Spirit of St. Louis" is a way cool plane. Charles Lindbergh helped design it, and then, in 1927, flew it nonstop from New York to Paris, all by himself. Amelia Earhart did the same thing five years later in her nifty red airplane. Score one for us girls!

Apollo 11 was the first manned mission to land on the moon. Neil Armstrong said, "That's one small step for man, one giant leap for mankind." We touched the moon rock on display. I thought it would make my fingers tingle, but it felt like a regular old Earth rock.

I loved the planetarium show. Glittery stars winked overhead . . . James said I snored! I told him I was daydreaming about flying my own plane.

Your starry-eyed daughter,
Olivia

On the ninth day of Christmas, my cousin gave to me . . .

9 airplanes flying

8 wacky statues, 7 drafters dancing, 6 frisky squirrels, 5 dollar bills, 4 monuments, 3 cute bears, 2 ruby slippers, and a thrush in a scarlet oak tree.

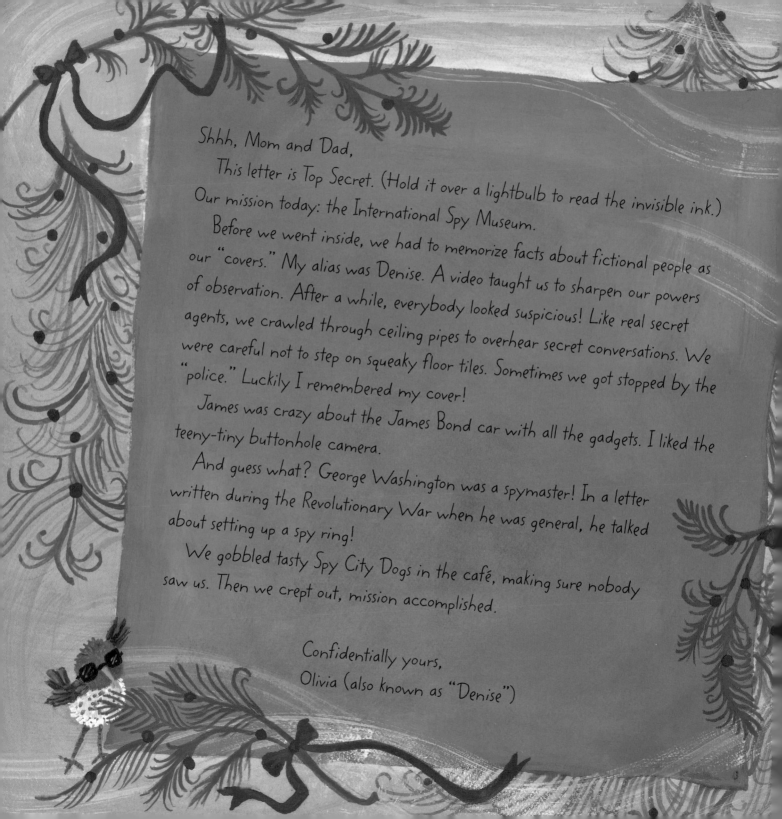

Shhh, Mom and Dad,

This letter is Top Secret. (Hold it over a lightbulb to read the invisible ink.)

Our mission today: the International Spy Museum.

Before we went inside, we had to memorize facts about fictional people as our "covers." My alias was Denise. A video taught us to sharpen our powers of observation. After a while, everybody looked suspicious! Like real secret agents, we crawled through ceiling pipes to overhear secret conversations. We were careful not to step on squeaky floor tiles. Sometimes we got stopped by the "police." Luckily I remembered my cover!

James was crazy about the James Bond car with all the gadgets. I liked the teeny-tiny buttonhole camera.

And guess what? George Washington was a spymaster! In a letter written during the Revolutionary War when he was general, he talked about setting up a spy ring!

We gobbled tasty Spy City Dogs in the café, making sure nobody saw us. Then we crept out, mission accomplished.

Confidentially yours,
Olivia (also known as "Denise")

On the tenth day of Christmas,
my cousin gave to me . . .

10 agents spying

9 airplanes flying, 8 wacky statues, 7 drafters dancing,
6 frisky squirrels, 5 dollar bills, 4 monuments,
3 cute bears, 2 ruby slippers,
and a thrush in a scarlet oak tree.

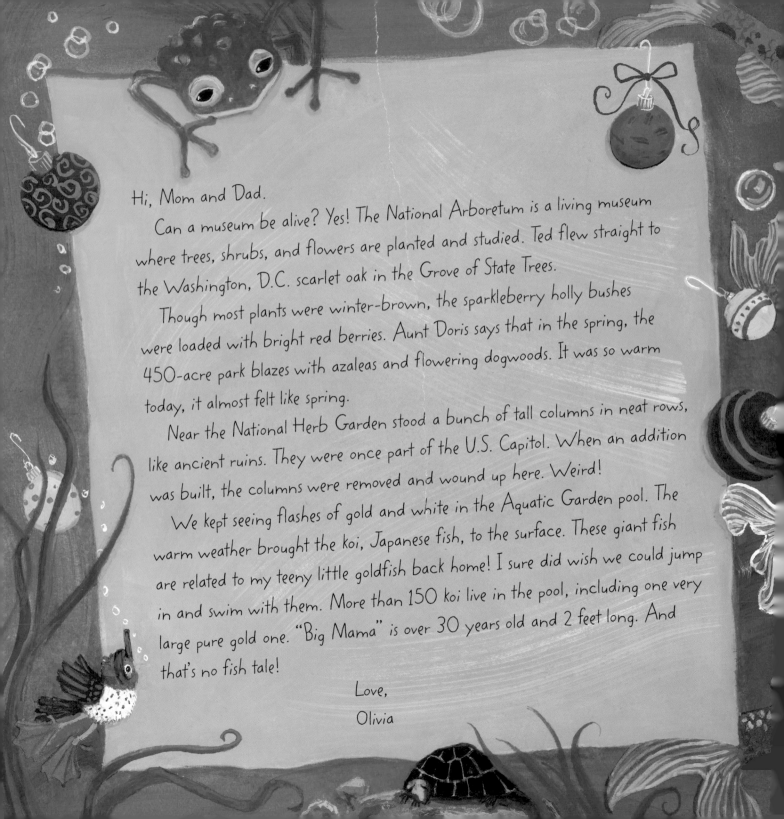

Hi, Mom and Dad.

Can a museum be alive? Yes! The National Arboretum is a living museum where trees, shrubs, and flowers are planted and studied. Ted flew straight to the Washington, D.C. scarlet oak in the Grove of State Trees.

Though most plants were winter-brown, the sparkleberry holly bushes were loaded with bright red berries. Aunt Doris says that in the spring, the 450-acre park blazes with azaleas and flowering dogwoods. It was so warm today, it almost felt like spring.

Near the National Herb Garden stood a bunch of tall columns in neat rows, like ancient ruins. They were once part of the U.S. Capitol. When an addition was built, the columns were removed and wound up here. Weird!

We kept seeing flashes of gold and white in the Aquatic Garden pool. The warm weather brought the koi, Japanese fish, to the surface. These giant fish are related to my teeny little goldfish back home! I sure did wish we could jump in and swim with them. More than 150 koi live in the pool, including one very large pure gold one. "Big Mama" is over 30 years old and 2 feet long. And that's no fish tale!

Love,
Olivia

On the eleventh day of Christmas, my cousin gave to me . . .

11 giant goldfish

10 agents spying, 9 airplanes flying, 8 wacky statues,
7 drafters dancing, 6 frisky squirrels, 5 dollar bills,
4 monuments, 3 cute bears, 2 ruby slippers,
and a thrush in a scarlet oak tree.

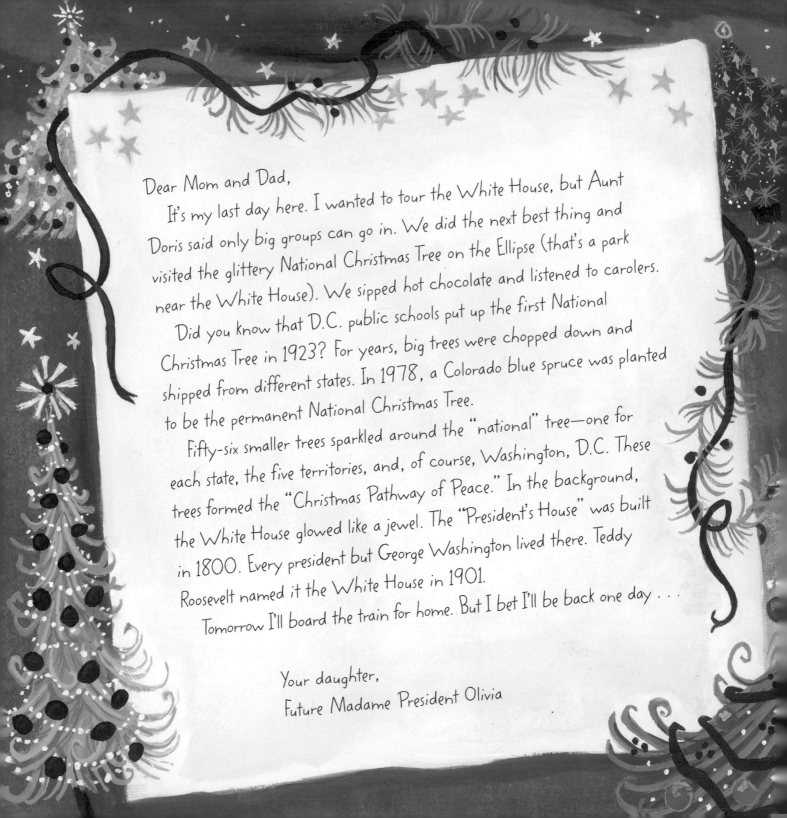

Dear Mom and Dad,

It's my last day here. I wanted to tour the White House, but Aunt Doris said only big groups can go in. We did the next best thing and visited the glittery National Christmas Tree on the Ellipse (that's a park near the White House). We sipped hot chocolate and listened to carolers.

Did you know that D.C. public schools put up the first National Christmas Tree in 1923? For years, big trees were chopped down and shipped from different states. In 1978, a Colorado blue spruce was planted to be the permanent National Christmas Tree.

Fifty-six smaller trees sparkled around the "national" tree—one for each state, the five territories, and, of course, Washington, D.C. These trees formed the "Christmas Pathway of Peace." In the background, the White House glowed like a jewel. The "President's House" was built in 1800. Every president but George Washington lived there. Teddy Roosevelt named it the White House in 1901.

Tomorrow I'll board the train for home. But I bet I'll be back one day . . .

Your daughter,
Future Madame President Olivia

On the twelfth day of Christmas,
my cousin gave to me . . .

12 sparkly pine trees

11 giant goldfish, 10 agents spying, 9 airplanes flying,
8 wacky statues, 7 drafters dancing, 6 frisky squirrels,
5 dollar bills, 4 monuments, 3 cute bears, 2 ruby slippers,
and a thrush in a scarlet oak tree.

Wonderful Wash

COME BACK SOON!

We the People of the

Presidential Inauguration Parade

AVERAGE TEMPERATURES
January: 35°F
July: 88°F

Fourth of July Celebration

OCTAGON HOUSE
Temporary White House after burning of Washington in 1814

"Friendship Archway" to Chinatown has 300 painted dragons!

Annual White House Easter Egg Roll

National Frisbee Festival

Butterfly Garden at the U.S. Botanic Garden

Lisa Halaby, married King Hussein of Jordan and became Queen Noor

WEST SIDE STORY
Chita Rivera, dancer, actress

Goldie Hawn
Academy Award® winning actress

John F. Kennedy Jr.
1960–1999

Connie Chung, Journalist and TV an

Washington, D.C.: The Nation's Capital

Abbreviation: D.C. (The District of Columbia) • **Bird:** the wood thrush •
Flower: the American Beauty rose • **Tree:** the scarlet oak • **Song:**
"The Star-Spangled Banner" • **Motto:** "Justice to All" • **Sports Teams:**
Redskins (football), Nationals (baseball), Wizards (basketball), Capitals (hockey)

Some Famous Washingtonians:

Alexander Graham Bell (1847-1922) was best known for inventing the telephone. In the early 1880s, he set up a laboratory in Washington, D.C. As president of the National Geographic Society, it was his idea to add photographs and lively writing to the magazine.

Mary William Ethelbert Appleton "Billie" Burke (c. 1887-1970) starred on the stage, in movies, and even had her own radio show. She married Florenz Ziegfeld Jr., producer of spectacular musicals. She is best known for her role as Glinda the Good Witch in the movie *The Wizard of Oz*.

Benjamin O. Davis (1877-1970) was the first African-American to rise to the rank of general in the U.S. Army. His son, **Benjamin O. Davis Jr.** (1912-2002) became the first African-American Air Force general. During World War II, he commanded the Tuskegee Airmen, an all-black unit of combat pilots. Father and son were born in Washington, D.C.

Edward Kennedy "Duke" Ellington (1899-1974) was a legendary jazzman, pianist, band leader and composer born in Washington, D.C. His orchestra played at the famous Cotton Club in Harlem, New York. He is best remembered for the tunes "Mood Indigo" and "It Don't Mean a Thing (If It Ain't Got That Swing)."

Helen Hayes (1900-1993), "The First Lady of Theater," began acting at the age of 5. In her 70-year career, this Washingtonian won an Emmy® (TV), a Grammy® (recording), an Oscar® (movie), and a Tony® (stage play) Award.

J(ohn) Edgar Hoover (1895-1972) was born on New Year's Day in Washington, D.C. He was appointed the first director of the Bureau of Investigation—predecessor to the FBI—in 1924. Hoover was instrumental in founding the FBI in 1935, where he remained director until his death in 1972.

John Philip Sousa (1854-1932) composed music for military bands. Born in Washington, D.C., "The March King" composed more than two hundred songs, operettas, and marches, including the rousing "Stars and Strips Forever."

To the city most tourists don't see: the real District of Columbia,
where people live and work and play and go to school. And to the city everyone—
rich or poor, young or old—can visit to enjoy the nation's treasures. Mostly for free!
—C.R.

To all the children who delight in visiting our wonderful city!
—S.H.

STERLING and the distinctive Sterling logo are registered trademarks of Sterling Publishing Co., Inc.

Library of Congress Cataloging-in-Publication Data
Ransom, Candice F., 1952-
The twelve days of Christmas in Washington, D.C. / written by Candice Ransom ; illustrated by Sarah Hollander.
p. cm.
Summary: Olivia writes a letter home each of the twelve days she spends exploring the nation's capitol at Christmastime, as her cousin James shows her everything from a wood thrush in a scarlet oak tree to twelve sparkly pine trees near the National Christmas Tree. Includes facts about Washington, D.C.
ISBN 978-1-4027-6394-6
1. Washington (D.C.) —Juvenile fiction. [1. Washington (D.C.) —Fiction. 2. Christmas—Fiction. 3. Cousins—Fiction. 4. Letters—Fiction.] I. Hollander, Sarah, ill. II. Title.
PZ7.R1743Twe 2010   [E] —dc22
2009010630

Lot#:
2 4 6 8 10 9 7 5 3 1
06/10

Published by Sterling Publishing Co., Inc.
387 Park Avenue South, New York, NY 10016
Text © 2010 by Candice Ransom
Illustrations © 2010 by Sarah Hollander
The original illustrations for this book were created in gouache.
Distributed in Canada by Sterling Publishing
C/o Canadian Manda Group, 165 Dufferin Street
Toronto, Ontario, Canada M6K 3H6
Distributed in the United Kingdom by GMC Distribution Services
Castle Place, 166 High Street, Lewes, East Sussex, England BN7 1XU
Distributed in Australia by Capricorn Link (Australia) Pty. Ltd.
P.O. Box 704, Windsor, NSW 2756, Australia

Sterling ISBN 978-1-4027-6394-6

For information about custom editions, special sales, premium and corporate purchases, please contact
Sterling Special SalesDepartment at 800-805-5489 or specialsales@sterlingpublishing.com.

Designed by Kate Moll.